Monday Popular Concerts.

DIRECTOR—Mr. S. ARTHUR CHAPPELL.

Four Hundred and Ninety-fourth Concert.*

PROGRAMME FROM THE WORKS OF

Various Masters.

MONDAY EVENING, DECEMBER 7th, 1874.

* Ninth Concert of the Seventeenth Season.

Part I

QUARTET, in C major, Op. 20, No. 2, for two Violins,
Viola, and Violoncello.   *Haydn.*

(First performance at the Popular Concerts.)

Moderato—C major.
Adagio—C minor; with Episode—E flat major.
Minuetto—C major; with Trio—C minor.
Allegro (Finale—Fuga a quattro suggetti)—C major.

Madame NORMAN-NÉRUDA,

Herr L. RIES, Mr. ZERBINI, and Signor PIATTI.

This quartet is, in many respects, one of the most original
and curious of the almost countless examples of chamber music
its inexhaustible composer has given to art. Each movement
has a strongly marked character of its own.

Moderato (leading theme).

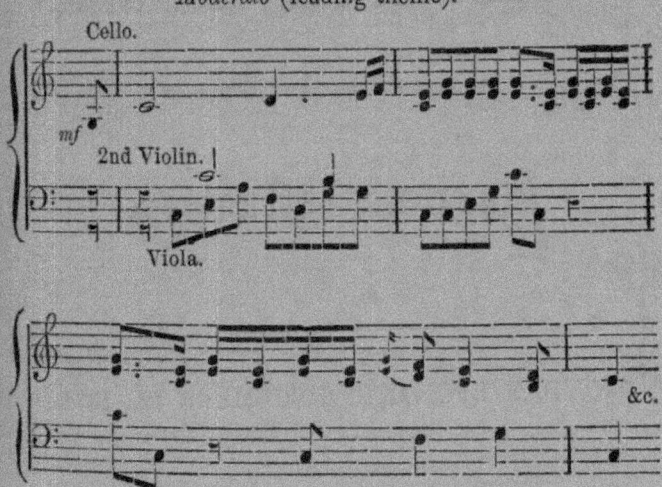

The first violin, hitherto tacit, now takes up the theme, in
the dominant :—

(Melody only.)

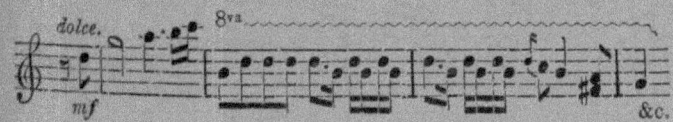

Again the second violin takes up the theme in the primary key, but with certain modifications :—

Thence we get speedily into the region of the orthodox dominant, as a preparation for the second theme.

This second theme is made up of a diversity of phrases, as, for example :—

And then, after a full close :—

Then again :—

Then once more :—

Then an episode in an extraneous key (E flat) :—

And, lastly, the playful peroration in the dominant (G) :—

The second part begins with an episode :—

—which, after being led through a variety of keys, gives way to some interesting development of the materials already cited. These return with some unimportant changes, after the accustomed manner. The episode to the second theme comes now in A flat (instead of E flat):—

(Melody only.)

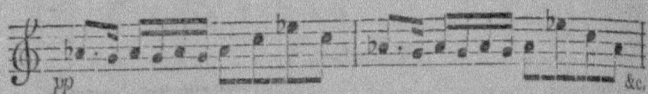

—and the movement thus tranquilly comes to a close.

The charm of this *moderato* lies in its exquisite and tuneful simplicity. Both first and second sections are intended by the composer to be repeated.

Adagio (leading theme).

The four instruments in unison.

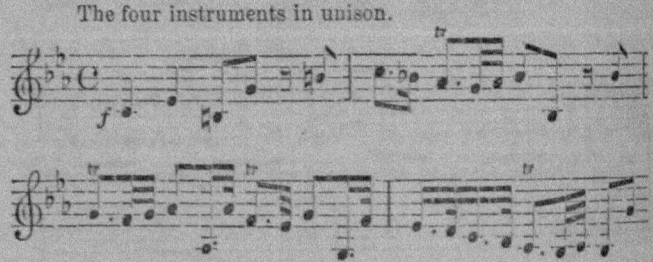

The violoncello then takes the theme:—

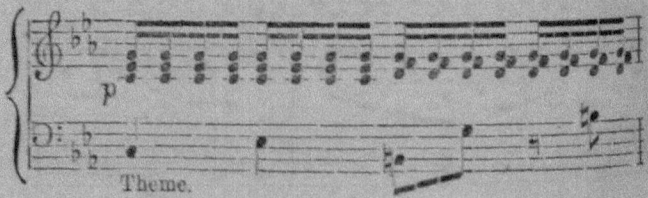

(Tributary.)

(Episode—E flat major.)

The Viola here plays an accompaniment of triplets in *arpeggio.*

It is not requisite to quote further from this brief, but
fine movement, in which Haydn makes freer use of unison
than is his ordinary custom. It does not come to a full close,
but breaks off on the harmony of the dominant, thus introducing the *minuetto*, in C major :—

Minuetto.

At the end of the first section of the *minuetto*, we have
again the four instruments in unison :—

Tutti.

Trio (C minor).

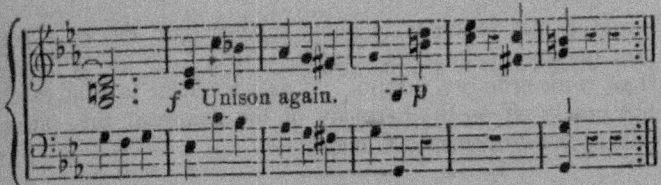

There is still further unison in the second part of this *trio*. Thus it begins :—

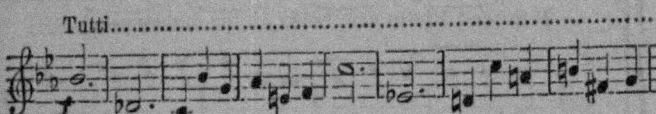

Like the *adagio* (which is in the same key), the *trio* leaves off on the dominant, when the *minuetto* is resumed in precisely the same manner.

The final *allegro* is a free but elaborately-conducted fugue, built upon the four themes subjoined :—

(First theme—First Violin.)

(Second theme—Viola.)

(Third theme—First Violin.)

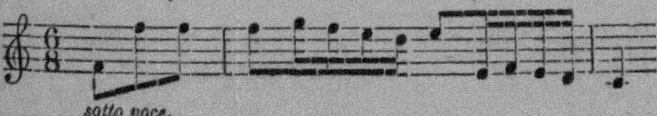

(Fourth theme—Viola.)

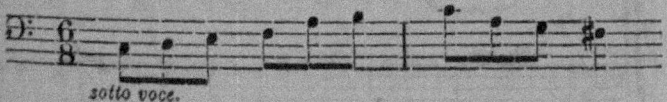

It will be observed that each theme begins on a different part of the bar. Theme 1 is answered, at the fourth bar, by the second violin, a fifth below :—

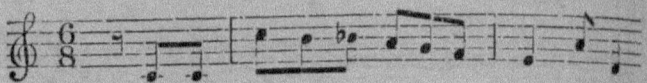

Theme 2, at the sixth bar, by the first violin, a fifth above :—

Theme 3, at the seventh bar, by the second violin, a fourth below :

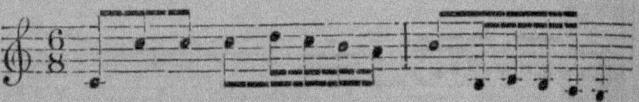

Theme 4, at the eighth bar, by the first violin, a fifth above :—

It should now be shown how Haydn makes them assort, as counterpoint to each other. Thus he sets out :—

To follow out the ramifications of the fugue to the end, with its sequences, episodes, and other devices of counterpoint, would be to little purpose. It is entirely constructed upon the foregoing materials. An episode immediately preceding the *coda*, in which the opening bar of the first of the four themes is first given by inversion, and answered direct:—

—afterwards imitated by the first and second violins :—

—will attract attention ; so, doubtless, will the *coda* itself :—

—which is carried on as brilliantly as it sets out; so will the passage on the dominant pedal (G) :—

—and so the snatches from all four themes :—

—leading to the vigorous unison for all the instruments, with which a movement almost unique in its kind is brought to an end:

Francis Joseph Haydn was born on the 21st of March, 1732, at Rhorau, and died on the 31st of May, 1809,* at Vienna, in his 79th year. Long as he lived, his productions are so numerous that they might reasonably account for a still more protracted career. The catalogue of his works which he drew up with his own hand, and presented to Carpani for the *Memoirs*, comprises upwards of eight hundred compositions of more or less importance. Besides his oratorios and masses, so well known to all musicians and amateurs in this country, Haydn composed twenty-four operas, one hundred and eighteen orchestral symphonies, and eighty-three quartets for stringed instruments. If he had written nothing but his quartets, he would have done quite enough—without oratorio, mass, opera, symphony, or canzonet—to render himself immortal. The number of his compositions for the chamber is prodigious, and as a whole they constitute one of the most varied and precious bequests to the art. They are otherwise interesting, moreover, for two special reasons; first, because the earlier examples exercised an undoubted influence in directing the studies and in forming the genius of Mozart; and, secondly, because the best of them show an ambition on the part of one who had been the model, and in a certain sense the master, to emulate the greatness of his still more gifted pupil and successor. It is an incident unique in the history of music, that Haydn, to whom Mozart owed so much, should afterwards have repaid himself with interest, by borrowing from the very source to which he had originally contributed. Every amateur knows what Mozart thought of Haydn; and every amateur equally knows what Haydn thought of Mozart.

* The year of Mendelssohn's birth, and fifty years subsequent to the death of Handel.

RECIT. and AIR, Mr. SIMS REEVES.

(Jephthah.)   *Handel.*

RECIT.

Deeper and deeper still thy goodness, child,
Pierceth a father's bleeding heart, and checks
The cruel sentence on my falt'ring tongue.
Oh! let me whisper it to the raging winds,
Or howling deserts; for the ears of men
It is too shocking.—Yet, have I not vow'd?
And can I think the great Jehovah sleeps,
Like Chemosh, and such fabled deities?
Ah! no! Heav'n heard my thoughts, and wrote them down.
It must be so—'Tis this that racks my brain,
And pours into my breast a thousand pangs
That lash me into madness.—Horrid thought!
My only daughter!—so dear a child,
Doom'd by a father!—Yes—the vow is pass'd,
And Gilead hath triumph'd o'er his foes.—
Therefore, to-morrow's dawn—I can no more.

AIR.

Waft her, angels, through the skies,
 Far above yon azure plain;
Glorious there, like you, to rise;
 There, like you, for ever reign.

From the oratorio of *Jephthah*, the last of Handel's sacred works*, commenced January 21, finished August 30, 1751, and produced February 26, 1752. Handel was 67 when he composed *Jephthah*, and it was while engaged on it that he was attacked with the *gutta serena* that deprived him of his sight. He lived more than seven years later, dying at the age of 74 years, one month and twenty-one days, on the 13th of April, 1759—a Good Friday, the anniversary of the first performance of *The Messiah*.

---

* *The Triumph of Time* (produced in 1757) was merely a revival with additions (an English version, of course) of the oratorio of *Il Trionfo del Tempo e Disinganno*, composed in Italy, half a century previous.

SONATA, in A flat major, Op. 110, for Pianoforte
alone. *Beethoven.*

(Fifth performance at the Popular Concerts.)

Moderato cantabile molto espressivo—A flat major.
Allegro molto—F minor; with episode—D flat major.

FINALE. { Adagio ma non troppo (Arioso dolente)—A flat minor.
Allegro ma non troppo (Fuga)—A flat major.
Tempo di Arioso—G minor.
Tempo della Fuga—G major; G minor;
and A flat major.

Mr. CHARLES HALLÉ.

In a letter addressed to his London publishers, the late
and well-known Carl Czerny of Vienna—an intimate friend
of Beethoven, to whose nephew he gave instructions on the
pianoforte—divides Beethoven's compositions into " periods,"
or styles, viz. "I. *The Haydn-Mozart style* (till the year
1802, and about as far as Op. 28) ; 2. *The strict Beethoven
style*—in all its original grandeur (from 1803 to 1815); 3.
The style which arose out of his deafness (from 1816 to 1826,
when he died)." That this arrangement by no means fitted
the pianoforte sonatas, is unquestionable ; but, perhaps, the
most flagrant instances of its inapplicability—or at least of
Czerny's erroneous system of applying it, is the classification
of the three sonatas, Ops. 109, 110, and 111 :—

"The following works, it is true, were completed by Beethoven,
and published during the same period (the third period) ; but their
conception and *origin* are decidedly of an earlier period, which may
be termed a *transition-period :*—1. Op. 109.—Sonata for piano solo
in E major ; 2. Op. 110.—Sonata for piano solo in A flat major;
3. Op. 111.—Sonata for piano solo in C minor. That these three
sonatas were commenced at a much earlier period, is not only
evident from the variety of style in the individual phrases, but also
from the circumstance that they were written for a small piano of
five-and-a-half-octaves only (for which Beethoven was in the habit
of writing in 1806), while all his last pianoforte sonatas are intended
for six-octave pianofortes."

Now, if we except the middle movement (*Prestissimo—*
in E minor) of " Op. 109," there is not a phrase but em-
phatically belongs to the " third period ; " while the last
movement (*Arietta*—with variations) of " Op. 111 " is in-
contestably of the same family. Of the work immediately
under notice (" Op. 110 "—A flat major), not one bar can
be traced either to the early or middle periods—to say
nothing about the plan of the sonata, which (if precedent
counts for anything) indelibly stamps it as a matured example
of the composer's latest manner. The leading theme is
divided into two sections. The first section is subjoined :—

Of the second it suffices to quote the melody:—

This is followed up by a brilliant passage of "tonic and dominant," in the *bravura* style:—

—the development of which prepares the way for a melodious introduction to the second subject, of which the opening is subjoined:—

3 A

—together with its still more engaging continuation :—

The second subject is one of the composer's wayward inspirations :—

The continuation, however, is extremely beautiful :—

—and brings the first part of the movement to a close, in the dominant (E flat) of the original key. The second part—thus concisely prefaced :—

—begins with an allusion to the leading theme—in F minor :—

—the harmony of the *six-four* being, at the end of the **crescendo**, thus unceremoniously abandoned :—

This new feature being worked out, we have a resumption of the leading theme, in the original key (A flat major), with another style of accompaniment :—

In this form the leading theme is developed at greater length than in the first part, in order that enough of A flat may be heard to balance the effect of an unexpected transition into an extraneous key. This transition is brought about by first giving the second section of the leading theme in D flat; and then, through an enharmonic change of D flat to C sharp, modulating to E:—

—in which key the brilliant passage now makes its appearance:—

All this time, it should be observed, we are in a wrong key—as if, almost, we had unknowingly got by some means into another sonata. Of this, "at the eleventh hour," Beethoven seems to be suddenly aware, and, as it were, conscience-stricken, hurries back (by a "short cut") to A flat:—

From this point the ordinary recapitulation goes on, until we arrive at a *coda*, in the course of which—as though to atone for having taken it so far from home—we are again presented with the twice-quoted brilliant passage—now in the key of **A** flat:—

One of the most striking points of the *coda* is the following:—

Thus, by long dwelling on the tonality of A flat, Beethoven artfully helps the ear to get rid of the impression created by the extraneous transition alluded to.

The *Allegro molto* (F minor), a *scherzo* in two-four measure, is of a wild and brusque character:—

The tributary of this theme is somewhat more melodious :—

The end of this part of the *Scherzo* is accompanied by another caprice of Beethoven's wayward fancy :—

The subject of the episode or trio (D flat major) is, to say the most of it, eccentric :—

When this quaint theme has been worked out (all on the pattern of the fragment cited), the *scherzo* (F minor) is resumed and given *notatim* as at first ; a brief *coda* (with further pauses) commencing thus :—

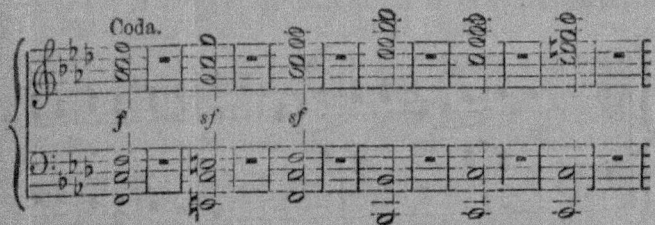

being the only new feature.

The *Finale* is not only by many degrees the finest part of the Sonata, Op. 110, but one of Beethoven's most original and beautiful inspirations. It is thoroughly dramatic, both in form and expression, and might indeed be aptly entitled *scena tragica*. Thus vaguely and mysteriously it sets out:—

After this, which might stand for orchestral symphony or prelude to the *scena*, a brief recitative suggests the entry of the voice. Then another interlude brings us, through an enharmonic transition, to the dominant of E, upon which some further recitative is constructed. Lastly, a transition back again from E to A flat minor concludes the recitative, as subjoined:—

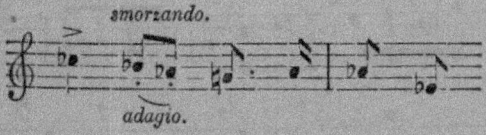

All this is preliminary to the *Arioso dolente* (A flat minor—*twelve-sixteen* measure), from which it will suffice to quote a fragment of the melody:—

Such pathos as is revealed in the progress of this *arioso* must speak eloquently for itself. It ends as impressively and solemnly as it begins. And now we have a striking example of Beethoven's consoling himself, in a mood of despondency, by the intellectual exercise of his art. The last bars of the *Arioso*—or rather the interlude that echoes its concluding notes :—

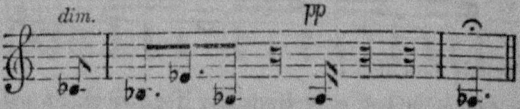

might have ended the movement and the sonata; for it would seem impossible to produce anything interesting after such an ebullition. The means of proceeding, however, were at command of the musician, who could, when it suited him, be Bach as well as Beethoven. Just as the *Arioso* comes direct from the heart, so does the richly developed fugue—of which the following is the subject :—

—spring from a free and ingenious exercise of the intellect. Extended over four pages, this masterly exhibition of contrapuntal skill at length breaks off upon the dominant of A flat—whence, through a bold transition :—

—we are conducted to G minor, in which new key, the *Arioso* :—

—with some modification, enhancing, if possible, its pathetic loveliness—is repeated. This being brought to a termination in G major, is succeeded by a wholly new development of the fugue, the subject of which is now presented by *inversion* (rising intervals falling, and falling intervals rising) :—

When the second answer has been worked out (the theme **in** the bass), we come to an episode, by augmentation :—

The subject of the episode, allotted to the left hand) first bar), is imitated *alla fugato*, by the right (second bar): which style of treatment is pursued for some time. The dotted crotchets, tied one to another, and which here constitute the melody, will be recognised as the subject in its original form (*not* inverted), now presented by *augmentation* (in other words, the length of every note being doubled). After eight bars of this, the theme of the episode is entrusted to the right hand, the principal subject of the fugue (still by *augmentation*) becoming the bass:—

After this fresh contrivance, a part of the episode is given by *diminution* (the duration of each note being lessened by one-half), and imitated in free " canon " :—

Then we have the same part of the episode (again by *diminution*) answered in the bass by free (not strict) *inversion* with the principal subject of the fugue—also inverted—as an inner part :—

The contrapuntal invention of the composer by this time apparently exhausted, we are introduced to a vigorous *coda*:—

The subject of the fugue having been freely developed, in combination with the fluent and melodious counterpoint of which the foregoing example may suggest an idea, leads to a close in A flat. To this succeeds a *codetta* :—

—which, wrought out with spirit and brilliancy, brings this very interesting sonata to an end.

The original MS. of the Sonata, Op 110—still preserved at Vienna—bears the following inscription in the composer's own handwriting :—" *Sonata von L. van Beethoven, am* 25*ten Decemb.* 1821."

The Sonata in A flat major was first introduced by Madame Arabella Goddard, at the twenty-fifth concert of the fifth season—May 11, 1863.

END OF THE FIRST PART.

_{*} Mr. CHARLES HALLÉ will perform on one of Messrs. JOHN BROADWOOD and SONS' Concert Grand Pianofortes.

———

Entr' Acte.

ON EDITING.*

By G. A. Macfarren.

This is the age of editing. In other times it was enough for some men to produce and others to admire; but now a third function with respect to art has come to be established, a third person stands between the artist and those to whom his work is addressed, and the editor so frequently presents himself that the world begins to consider that his office must be indispensable.

Now, there are three orders of editorship.

One takes upon itself the duty of purifying the text of an inaccessible author, and of presenting his works in a form as like to that in which he left them as documentary and traditional evidence, together with most intelligent conjecture, can enable him to do. The result of his labour is what may be styled a library copy, valuable for reference on all occasions, and an authority on any points that may possibly be disputed. Such an edition as this, of any work of literary or musical art, cannot be too highly treasured, and, in the case of true masterpieces, is desirable beyond estimate. Literature has fared better; but the debatable incidents in musical works are many, very many, and the means of deciding them are far beyond the reach of a vast majority of the persons who are interested in them. An editor of this class needs to exercise his discretion when there is the choice of two authorities of nearly equal value; for instance, there may be the autograph of a work and a printed copy of the first edition of the same. In many cases the reliability of the former is indisputable; but, in others, it may often happen that a composer has improved upon first intentions, either from the experience of performance, from the reconsideration of a phrase, or from any other cause. He will then naturally alter the parts from which his piece is to be sung or played, or he will alter the proof sheets if it is to be printed; but he will rarely run home from a rehearsal or a printing office to correct his original MS. When this happens, of necessity a copy of the first edition is a better guide for the editor than is even the handwriting of the composer; at least, so judged the Council of the Handel Society, in opposition to Mendelssohn, when they issued *Israel in Egypt*, under the editorship of the latter, who wished to

---

* From the *Musical Times*.

restore several points from the MS. that had been altered, obviously for improvement's sake, before the oratorio was first printed. Some of these points are so highly interesting, that one, at least, may be cited in support of the Council's decision, and in proof of the superiority of the printed over the written authority. Throughout the chorus, "And with the blast of Thy nostrils," Handel wrote the often-repeated phrase, "the waters were gathered," with the word "we-re" in two syllables, having four separate quavers for "wa-ters we-re;" but printed it, as we all know, with two joined quavers for the first syllable, and one quaver each for the other two.

Another order of editorship engages itself with expounding, so to speak, the original, and by the substitution perhaps of one word or one note for another, or by the change of punctuation, to make clear the sense of phrases which has been left doubtful by the author. To this order belong the countless array of Shaksperean commentators, who have amended away at the assumed obscurities of the original text, till, it is probable, the author himself might be unable to recognize some of his passages, and quite unable to understand them in the guise these worthies have given them. The punctuation of music consists in the slurs to indicate the phrasing, which supply the place of the commas, semicolons, and the like, of literature, which are almost as essential to the sense as the very words they divide and congregate. It is in this matter of slurring or phrasing that the works of many musicians, even among the most eminent, are sadly defective. A thoroughly cultivated reader can, of course, supply for himself the deficiencies of the copy; and, if he give an interesting rendering of the work, we are thankful to him, even though his views of the expression of a phrase perhaps differ from those of the man who wrote it. Such a rendering is scarcely to be improvised, but demands, in most cases, so intimate a knowldege of the music, on the part of the player, that it must indeed live again as vividly in his mind as it did in that of the composer. This, and only this, can qualify him to treat a phrase as if it were his own; and it is only under such treatment that any phrase can come forth with a natural air, and an unconstrained expression. A vast proportion of music needs several simultaneous executants, and it is not possible under any doctrine of chances, that all of these can at once extemporize the same reading. It is necessary, then, for an efficient performance, that some person consider what has here been defined as the punctuation of music, and that he correspondingly mark the several parts which are to be played together. Some editors, of the order in present consideration, stretch their duty to its very verge, if not break it by excess of tension; which are they who not only indicate how many notes are to be given in one breath, or in one bow, or without raising the fingers from a keyboard, but mark what notes are to be played loudly and what softly, what are to be detached and what conjoined, and thus give often a meaning to a phrase which is apart from the composer's intention, and is sometimes opposed to the natural tendency of the phrase itself. This kind of thing is admissible in performance, where the personality of the player may give interest to his erratic construction of a composer's meaning; but it should not be perpetuated in print, unless accompanied with a complete description of what was originally written, and of what has been altered from and what added to the author's text. The free-handed and unavowed substitution of words in the edition of Shakspere that preceded the present generation, has led to the adoption of many of these in general belief as authentic, and it is only readers who make first acquaintance with the text from later editions, the principle of which is to restore the earliest readings, who can receive these unprejudiced by the powerful influence of familiarity with "amended" versions, which prompts the supposition that right is wrong and corruption is purity. So too, in the reprints of the masterpieces in music, it has been so far customary for editors to insert their own marks of piano and forte, and sforzando, and so forth, that when one lights upon a primitive copy, one is astonished to find how much and how little belong to the composer of these expressive directions. What may be styled a practical copy is of great use, of musical works, to players who have not the capabilities to interpret a composer's purpose by the light of their own intelligence, either for want of intimacy with a particular work, or of time to acquire it, when general education may perhaps have prepared them to obtain an insight into its design and details. Respect to convenience readers is often impracticable to define in print exactly what is editorial and what is authoritative; but it is of the highest importance that editions thus ornamented, let us admit it to be, with the annotations of an editor, should be distinguished as such, so that they may not mislead a reader into the supposition that the inserted marks are due to the writer of the piece. Let such as this be styled a school edition, if you will, and let its advantages be fully acknowledged; but let it never be confounded with the library edition before noticed, which there surely ought to exist, of every work whose interest was sufficient to make a knowledge desirable of what the author wrote, even though readers should in some instances prefer to depart therefrom. An edition of the pianoforte works of Beethoven, now in the course of issue in Germany, carries this assumed prerogative of an editor to an extent happily extraordinary, and extraordinary let us hope it may long continue. In this, with most reckless disregard of evidence, the editors, and one in particular, assume to have a kind of second sight of the author's meaning, and by the guidance of this preternatural light, they take upon themselves to set aside what Beethoven wrote and printed, and they supersede this in many passages by substitutions of their own, which materially change the character and alter the effect of what common-place folks blindly believe must have been intended by the master—poor common-place folks! who have but the indisputable notes of the original, the general manner of the author, a comprehension of the theoretical and practical state of art in his time, and a reverence for a great man's meaning and his individual way of expressing it, to guide them. They who are responsible for this edition, unscrupulously add octaves or double octaves to passages written in single notes, extend scales from one octave to two, and make other still more serious changes, which, let us do them the kindness to suppose, they imagine to be betterings of what the world received, as perfect prior to the pretence of these gentlemen to prove it to be imperfect. Of a totally different character, is an edition of the pianoforte sonatas recently issued in England, wherein infinite pains have been spent in purifying the text according to the highest authorities, and impunctuating the phrases as aforesaid, so as to distinguish their meaning to all who read them. The English, or one produced in the same spirit and with the same amount of insight, should of course be the school edition. The German edition must be a curiosity from which reason and feeling will revolt.

Our third order of editorship assumes the right and presumes the capability to add to the works of great musicians in order to fit them for present use. In letters the same was done by John Dryden, by Nahum Tate, and by David Garrick, with regard to the plays of Shakspere, and a pretty business they made of their changements. Mankind has come to the convictions that the Tempest is best without having a youth that has never seen a maiden; that King Lear is not improved by the omission of the Fool or by the love of Edgar and Cordelia; and that Romeo and Juliet is good enough without the waking of the heroine before her lover's death and a maudlin, dawdling, sentimental piece of whining in consequence between the two. Would that a like conviction with regard to music might break upon us! The names of an artist who wrote a Tragedy of four hours long, or an Oratorio of five—such as Hamlet or Belshazzar—could scarcely, with justice, rise from his repose to complain of the inevitable curtailment of his work; for now it is impossible, if ever an audience could endure it, to attend to a performance of such great extent. To shorten, where this is unavoidable, is one thing; to colour, to decorate, to misrepresent, or even to dress (when the applied costume is out of the fashion of the age to which the work belongs) is entirely another. Perhaps one of the greatest evils that have ever been done in music, is the reinstrumentation by Mozart of Handel's Messiah; and the evil lies in the fact that the score is written with such consummate artistry as to rival the beauty of the original matter, that it is hence inseparable (save in those pieces in which, from the first, Mozart's additions have been unused) from Handel's groundwork in public performances. Because of its infinite merit, Mozart's orchestration is now indispensable; and, because of its indispensability, any one now regards it as a precedent, and takes licence from its example to invest other works of Handel with "additional accompaniments." Unhappily, or happily, as the case may be, everybody who paints Handel with the vivid colours of the modern orchestra is not Mozart. If he were, and were always at his best, then should we become strangers to the effects intended by the mighty one of Halle, the stern grandeur and the special sweetness of the Saxon giant would have no existence, and the delicious haze of sunset glories that hangs as a kind of veil between the ancient style of music and the modern would hide from view the most salient features of the master's individuality. I plead guilty to this act of treason against the musician's memory in my own poor strivings, which would not be extenuated by a recital of the circumstances that induced me to the act; I but acknowledge that I live in a glass-pouse, and the stones I may throw will shatter as much my own panes as they may strike against the crystals of others. Now the case of Handel differs from that of every later musician, and, to a great extent, from that of some composers of his own period, in that the unwritten organ part formed a prominent and important feature in the performances over which he himself presided; and the absence of this designedly conspicuous feature, causes a vast blank, which imperatively needs to be filled. It was this imperative need which caused Mozart to write his wind instruments and occasionally to add to the string parts of Handel, for the performance of the Messiah in Vienna, in

a ball that had no organ. He must be a man with the genius of
Mozart or of Handel himself, or else with the belief that he had it,
who would now-a-days dare to improvise an organ part to any
work by Handel, that should aim at the contrapuntal character
and the general fulness of interest of what Handel is recorded to
have played; but a thing may be accomplished in the stillness of
contemplation, which is impossible in the heat of excitement, and
thus one—who could by no means extemporise it—might write, in
a fortunate humour, such an organ part as even Handel might not
have rejected. This would not be to modernise a work written in
the spirit of another age, but to fill up the gap occasioned by the
author's incomplete mode of writing. So deemed Mendelssohn—
more wisely than when he recast Acis and Galatea—when afterwards he wrote his truly Handelian organ part for Israel in
Egypt. It is seemingly inconsistent, on the other hand, to fill up
the incompleteness of Handel with instrumental effects such as he
never could have conceived, even though it be done after the
example of Mozart's Messiah. Let us pass on, however, to a
master who lived two generations after the grand old Colossus became silent, after the modern had been introduced into music by
the magical touch of Mozart, and who is duly accredited with a
mastery over the materials wherewith he worked, that is equal to the
the measureless greatness of his thoughts. It has been proposed—
mercy measure the monstrocity!—to improve the orchestration of
the Choral Symphony of Beethoven, and the notion has been justly
met by Mr. Manns in a paragraph in the book of his benefit concert last April, and by Mr. Joseph Bennett in an article that ap-
peared in this journal. There is one thing to be urged, and this is
the single one, in support of the extravagant proposal—namely,
that let be written what may, either in the way of making clear the
ideas which Beethoven is now declared to have been unable to ex-
press, or else in making clear what the proposer would like him to
have expressed, let be written what may, the world has always the
freedom to receive or to reject it, and we who have full faith in
Beethoven, so may still play him as he wrote, and may still believe
that his writing is the immortal portion of himself. The orchestration of a master is as entirely individual to him as are his harmonies or his melodies. One can tell at a hearing that this or
that is a score of Mendelssohn or of Schumann, of Spohr or of
Weber, of Beethoven or of Mozart, quite as certainly as one can
recognise a painter by his colouring, or a poet by his idiom. Would
a passage by Shakespere be any longer his, were every word in it
that is unusual in our times to be replaced by the last new Uni-
versity slang phrase which has been adopted by the Girl of the
Period? Would a picture by Reynolds be any longer his, were it
to be recoloured by even the ablest of living artists? Let it be
granted that some of the orchestral effects of our master are not
satisfactory to the full, and let it be presumed that this is a possible
consequence of his infirmity, which he might have altered had he
heard these effects as we hear them. What then? If Beethoven
had not possessed that miraculous inner sense of sound through
which he perceived the beautiful, he would not have been Beethoven;
and, in like manner, had he not possessed that natural as lament-
able outer senselessness to the very sounds of his own conceptions,
so neither would he have been Beethoven. It is he that is our love,
our adoration; and he, disguised by the manipulation of another

hand, at the prompting of another brain, is a stranger to musicians, and strange may he be for ever. It is argued that the capabilities of instruments have been extended since our master wrote, and that he would have constructed different passages had the means been at hand for their execution. What then? Had he written something else, he would not have written what he wrote, and we shall better enjoy this legacy of genius if we believe it to be unimprovable, than if we submit it to the hacking mercies of any aftercomer. Nay, the then limitation of compass of certain instruments brought particular beauties into some works of Beethoven which would not have been there had pianofortes and flutes and other machines for setting the air in motion been without top or bottom to their scale. Notice in testimony, the many incidents, in the early Sonatas particularly, which, recurring in different keys from those wherein they first are heard, are then modified to bring them within the bounds of the instrument that would have been exceeded had the said incidents been precisely transposed; and new beauties spring from these modifications, beauties that never would have come into being had the copyist instead of the composer been able to transfer the phrases unaltered from one key into another. Let it be granted, a grant beyond the amplitude of all heretofore concessions, that the passages it is proposed to alter are weak, unworthy, even faulty. What then? A true lover may perceive faults in the person, or the mind, or the character of his mistress; but will he love her the less? Will he not love her in spite of, and even because of these imperfections? This order of editorship has received countenance and even support in English print. Alas and well-a-day! It becomes then a duty to protest against it; but no protest can obliterate a once printed word. It is the winged seed that is borne upon the air from clime to clime and from people to people; there is only to wish, where hope has no anchor, that the seed may fall on flinty soil, and that men's hearts will afford no nurture to the art-impiety. May such never become the concert edition of musical classics.

The responsibility of a musical editor is beyond calculation. We owe an infinite debt of gratitude to anyone who accepts this responsibility with implicit faith in his author; we owe as deep a debt of resentment to one who grasps it with an unshakeable belief in himself.

Part II.

~~~~~~~~~~~~~~~~~~~~~~~~~~~~~~~~~~~~~~~

SONATA, in F major, for Violoncello, with Pianoforte
Accompaniment. *Marcello.*

(First performance at the Popular Concerts.)

Largo—F major.
Allegro—F major.
Largo—D minor.
Presto—F major.

Signor PIATTI.

(Pianoforte, Sir JULIUS BENEDICT.)

For the pianoforte accompaniment to this sonata we are
indebted to Signor Piatti himself, who has arranged it from
the figured bass of the composer.

Adagio.

Allegro.

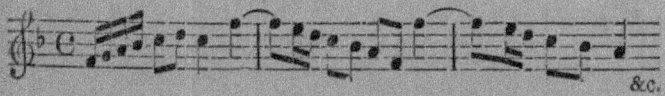

Largo (D minor).

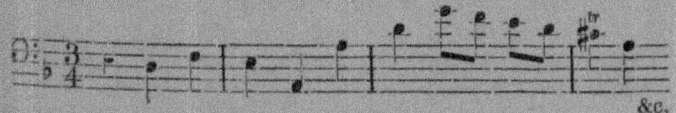

Presto.

&

Benedetto Marcello was born in Venice in 1686, of one of the noblest families of that republic. His musical compositions were very numerous, consisting of psalms, operas, madrigals, and songs. He was also a poet, and wrote several of the dramatic pieces which he set to music. His great work, still well known to musicians, is his *Psalms*. It is a paraphrase of the first fifty Psalms, written by Ascanio Giustiniani, and set to music in one, two, and three vocal parts, by Marcello, published in 1724 and 1725. There is a fine English edition of this work, in eight folio volumes, which was set on foot by Mr. Avison, author of the *Essay on Musical Expression,* and accomplished by Mr. Garth, of Durham, who adapted to the music words from our prose translation of the Psalms. Marcello's Psalms have received more and less than justice from different critics. While Avison's praise is somewhat exaggerated, Burney's censure is too severe. Burney ascribes the "over praise" which Marcello received, partly, at least, to his nobility; but however much this consideration may have operated during his life, it can hardly account for the elevated rank which has been assigned to him as a musician, by the greatest writers on the art. It is enough to mention Padre Martini, of Bologna, who, in his celebrated *Saggio di Contrapunta* (Essay on Counterpoint), mentions Marcello as one of the greatest masters of the Venetian school. The work in question is certainly worthy of the author's reputation. It is full of beautiful and expressive melodies; the contexture of the vocal parts is admirable; and there is great boldness and variety in the modulations and harmonies. The music, however, is somewhat too light and dramatic; it is defective in the severe simplicity and grave solemnity which ought to characterise the ecclesiastical style. Marcello's *Psalms* have now become a rare book; but extracts are to be found in different collections of sacred music; and some movements of them are occasionally heard at concerts.

Among Marcello's literary productions, which are numerous, there is a satire, entitled *Teatro alla moda*, or, "An easy and certain method of composing and performing Italian operas after the modern manner." It is amusing to observe how pointedly the sarcasms against the *modern* fashions of 1720 are applicable to the modes of our own day.

The satire is levelled against poets as well as composers. "The modern poet," says the author, "should completely abstain from reading the ancient writers; for this reason, that the ancient writers never read the moderns. Before entering upon his task, he will take an exact note of the quantity and quality of the scenes which the manager is desirous of introducing into his drama. He will compose his poem verse by verse, without giving himself any trouble as to the action, in order that it may be impossible for the spectator to comprehend the plot, and that curiosity may thus be kept alive to the end of the piece. By the way, he will not forget to close the piece with a brilliant and magnificent scene, terminating in a grand chorus in honour of the sun, the moon, or the manager. He will have recourse as frequently as possible to the dagger, to poison, to earthquakes, spectres, and incantations. All these expedients are admirable; they cost but little, and produce a prodigious effect on the public."

The satirist thus instructs the composer :—" The modern composer has no occasion for a knowledge of the rules of composition; practice, and a few general principles, will be quite sufficient. Nor has he any occasion for an acquaintance with poetry; he need not even be able to distinguish a long syllable from a short one. He will do well *not* to read the poem before setting it to music, for fear of overloading his imagination and oppressing his genius. He will compose the music verse by verse, and will not fail to adjust to the words such airs as he has composed in the course of the year, even though the metre and the expression should be at perfect variance with his ideas. He will produce no airs but such as are accompanied by the whole orchestra; for, in order to compose in the modern taste, it is indispensable above all things to make plenty of noise. As to the singers, they should take care never to practise sol-fa-ing, for fear of falling into the old-fashioned custom of singing in tune and time, both which things are at absolute variance with the taste of the day. And not only will they change the *time* of the airs, but also the airs themselves, though their variations are in direct opposition to the bass and the whole of the instruments."

Any "*laudator temporis acti*" of our own day, wishing to expose the present vices of the musical stage, in regard to poetry, composition, and performance, would handle the subject exactly as Marcello did above a century ago. He would talk of the degradation of the musical drama by its conversion into a spectacle *full of spectors and incantations*; of the determination of the composers, above all things, *to make plenty of noise*; and of the unmeaning and vicious flourishes with which the airs are loaded by uneducated singers; and he would recall with a sigh, the golden days when the Italian opera flourished in all its beauty and purity. And yet it was in those very golden days that Marcello's satire was written —in the days when Apostolo Zeno was in his zenith, and Metastasio was appearing on the horizon—when the music of the Italian stage was composed by Leo, Vinci, Porpora, Steffani, and Clari, and sung by Faustina, Cuzzoni, Caffarelli, and Farinelli. At a period, too, considerably later, but still at a time when the Italian school retained much of the excellence which it is now universally admitted to have lost, we find, in the correspondence of Metastasio,* the same complaints of the ignorance and bad taste of his contemporaries, and the same regretful looking back to past days, in which Marcello indulged before him, in which we indulge after him, and in which our posterity will indulge after us, so long as human nature shall remain what it is.

Marcello, notwithstanding his devotion to music and poetry, held important offices in the state, and was distinguished for his activity in the discharge of his public duties. He died at Brescia, in 1739.

---

* See Burney's *Life of Metastasio.*

SONG, Mr. SIMS REEVES. *Schubert.*

The English Words by SIR WALTER SCOTT.

Ave Maria! maiden mild!
  Listen to a maiden's prayer ;
Thou canst hear, though from the wild ;
  Thou canst save amid despair.
Safe may we sleep beneath thy care,
  Though banished, outcast, and reviled.
O, Maiden ! hear a maiden's prayer ;
  Mother, hear a suppliant child !
          Ave Maria !

Ave Maria ! undefil'd !
  The flinty couch we now must share
Shall seem with down of eider pil'd,
  If thy protection hover there.
The murky cavern's heavy air
  Shall breathe of balm, if thou hast smil'd ;
Then, Maiden ! hear a maiden's prayer ;
  Mother, list a suppliant child !
          Ave Maria !

Ave Maria ! stainless styl'd !
  Foul demons of the earth and air,
From this their wonted haunt exil'd,
  Shall flee before thy presence fair.
We bow us to our lot of care ;
  Beneath thy guidance reconcil'd.
Hear, for a maid, a maiden's prayer !
  And for a father, hear a child !
          Ave Maria !

This universally popular song is one of five set to German versions of the lyrics in Sir Walter Scott's *Lady of the Lake.* Its original title was " *Hymne an die Jungfrau.*" The five songs, of which this one is the fourth, were composed in 1825, and published by Artaria (Vienna) in 1826, as " Op. 52."

———

TRIO, in F major, Op. 28, for Pianoforte, Violin, and
Violoncello. *F. Gernsheim.*

(First performance at the Popular Concerts.)

Allegro ma non troppo—F major.
Scherzo, allegro molto vivace—B flat major ; with
Trio—B flat minor.
Largo—D minor ; leading to
Finale, allegro moderato assai—F major.

Mr. CHARLES HALLÉ, Mme. NORMAN-NÉRUDA,
and Signor PIATTI.

This trio, by one of the most promising composers of
"Young Germany," is constructed after the most approved
classic models. The plan of each of its four movements is so
clear and symmetrical that a citation of some of the leading
themes and episodes will answer all purposes.

The leading theme of the *allegro ma non troppo* is led off
by the violin and violoncello, in octaves :—

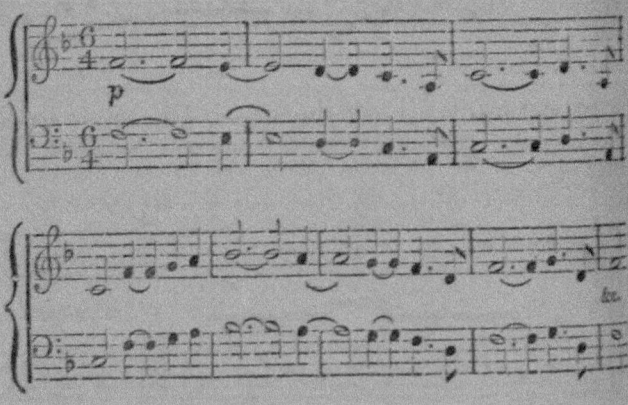

This is accompanied on the pianoforte by full chords, occurring at the two unaccented parts of each bar:—

At the full close the pianoforte takes up the theme, thus:—

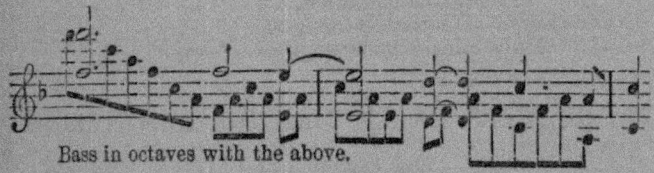

Bass in octaves with the above.

—the stringed instruments answering as below:—

The full close is put off by an interrupted cadence, which introduces the preliminary to the second theme—in D major:—

cadence.

—thus developed further on :—

cantabile.
Cello.

(Second theme.)

Cello.

This is shortly followed by a tributary, which forms the peroration of the first part of the movement, the shortest possible reference to which will suffice :—

The first part ends in this key (D), and is not repeated. The second part, or "free *fantasia*," in which all the materials quoted are brought together, will speak for itself. One episode, however, built upon the original theme, is worth particular attention :—

In octaves with the right hand.

In the preceding quotations the entire *allegro* may be seen. No more need be cited till we arrive at the *coda*, which, beginning as subjoined :—

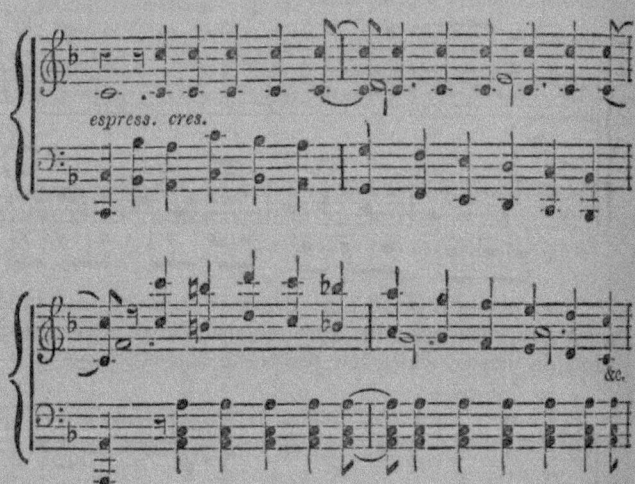

—contains further references to the themes already quoted.

The *scherzo* (B flat major) is exclusively constructed upon the subjoined theme :—

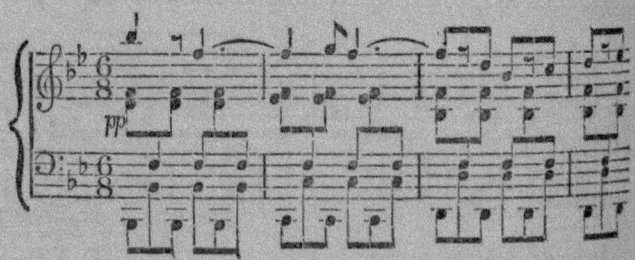

The violoncello then takes up the theme, to the same form of pianoforte accompaniment :—

The trio (*meno mosso*), in two-four measure, and in the minor key, sets out with a theme for the stringed instruments, in unison, which the pianoforte carries out :—

334

After the *trio*, the *scherzo* is repeated, without modification.

The *largo* consists of two themes—one in the minor key, and one in the major, both developed at considerable length.

(Leading theme—D minor.)

Episode—D major).

This movement does not come to a full close, but, through a transition, which must speak for itself, leads to the *finale*, of which the leading theme is subjoined:—

Then the violin, violoncello, and pianoforte, play a sort of imitative trio upon the theme, the accompaniment going on in triplets, as before :—

When this is worked out, we have an episode, beginning in the tonic key (F major) :—

The principle episode (or second theme) appears in the key of A major. The melody alone, led off by the violin, need be quoted; the accompaniment of plain chords in *arpeggio* will speak for itself:—

(Second theme.)

The violoncello then takes up the melody, the violin holding sustained notes, and the pianoforte accompaniment continuing in the same strain.

The theme is then submitted to contrapuntal treatment in the free imitative style :—

All the foregoing materials are made further use of in the course of this movement (which is in the *rondo* form), and no further quotation is necessary, till we arrive at the *coda*, which sets out, "*un poco più animato*," as below :—

FRITZ GERNSHEIM, born at Worms (on the Rhine) in 1839, is the son of a well-known physician. He left Worms

3 E

for Frankfort-on-the-Maine, where he studied the pianoforte under Edward Rosenhain (brother to Jacques Rosenhain, once well known in England), at the same time taking lessons in harmony and counterpoint from Hauff, a professor held in some esteem. From Frankfort he went to Leipsic, and became a pupil at the Conservatorium of that famous musical city. He then visited Paris, and subsequently accepted the post of musical director at Saarbrücken. At one period (at Mayence) he studied the pianoforte under the superintendence of Herr Ernst Pauer, whom, happily, we all know in England. He is now at Cologne, where, since 1865, he has established himself as a professor of music; but it is stated that he has lately accepted a post of some distinction at Rotterdam. Young as he is, Herr Gernsheim has already made a name for himself; and, if the trio performed to-day may be accepted as a criterion, he has a bright future before him.

———

END OF THE FOUR HUNDRED AND NINETY-FOURTH CONCERT.

———

J. MALLETT, PRINTER, 59, WARDOUR STREET, SOHO. W.

SATURDAY POPULAR CONCERTS.

SATURDAY AFTERNOON, DEC. 12th, 1874.

PROGRAMME.

QUARTET, in A major, Op. 18, No. 5, for two Violins, Viola, and Violoncello...*Beethoven.*

Madame NORMAN-NÉRUDA,

MM. L. RIES, ZERBINI, and PIATTI.

SONG, "I pray thee by the gods above" ....*Alwyn.*

Mr. SANTLEY.

SONATA, in G major, Op. 29, No. 1, for Pianoforte alone ....*Beethoven.*

Mr. CHARLES HALLÉ.

RECIT. and AIR, "Revenge, Timotheus cries." ....*Handel.*

(By desire.)

Mr. SANTLEY.

TRIO, in B flat, Op. 99, for Pianoforte, Violin, and Violoncello ....*Schubert.*

Mr. CHARLES HALLÉ, Madame NORMAN-NÉRUDA,

and Signor PIATTI.

Conductor - Sir JULIUS BENEDICT.

3 F

www.ingramcontent.com/pod-product-compliance
Lightning Source LLC
Chambersburg PA
CBHW081215170626
46811CB00010B/3305